BUS ROUTE TO
BOSTON

MARYANN COCCA-LEFFLER

Acknowledgments

I would like to thank George Sandborn, Reference Librarian at the Massachusetts State Transportation Library; Aaron Schmidt from the Boston Public Library Print Department; Filenes Basement, Inc.; Maria A. Stuto, teacher of Italian; and Marty Lundquist and his newspaper collection.

Published by Caroline House
Boyds Mills Press, Inc.
A Highlights Company
815 Church Street
Honesdale, Pennsylvania 18431
Printed in China

Publisher Cataloging-in-Publication Data

Cocca-Leffler, Maryann.
        Bus Route to Boston / by Maryann Cocca-Leffler. 1st ed.
[32]p. : col. ill. ;   cm.
Summary: An ordinary bus ride becomes a wonderful
adventure.
ISBN 1-56397-723-0
1. Boston--Juvenile fiction. [1. Boston--Fiction.] I. Title.
    [E]-dc21 2000 AC   CIP
98-88214

First edition, 2000
The text of this book is set in Bookman Medium.
The illustrations are done in acrylic on gessoed board.

10 9 8 7 6 5 4 3 2

To everyone who shares my memories of Woodlawn Avenue, Everett, Massachusetts, especially my parents, brothers, and sister. . . . and to those many MBTA bus drivers who travel in and out of Boston every day.

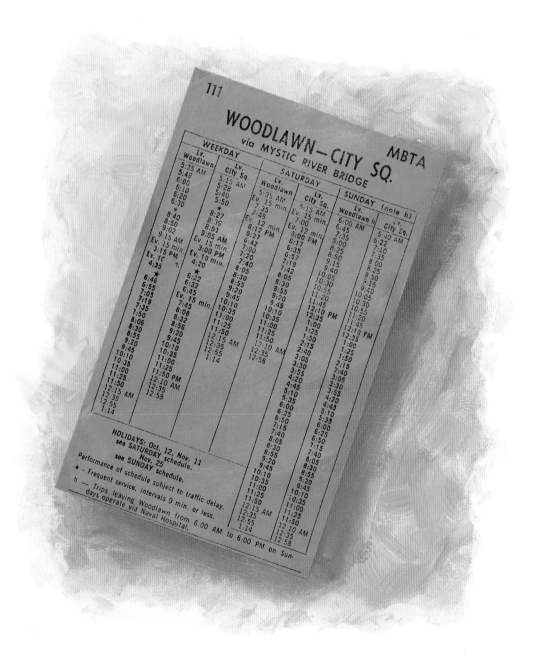

"BUS!" my little sister yelled.
We stopped our kickball game. Everyone
ran to the sidewalk to let the bus go by.
Bill, the bus driver, slowed down and waved.
"Who's winning?" he asked.

Our house was on a bus route. . . .

Every twenty minutes the bus traveled down our street,

over the bridge, then all the way into Boston.

Sometimes we would walk up to the corner, and Bill would give us a free ride down the street. We'd all sing the "Bus Song," and Bill would let us beep the horn.

But on Saturdays we got to take the bus all the way into Boston.

Last Saturday, Filene's Basement was having their big sale. There were crowds and crowds of shoppers. My little sister and I held hands so we wouldn't get lost. Mounds of clothes were everywhere. Mom dug through the piles to find the best bargains.

There were no dressing rooms. Ladies in their underwear crowded around the tiny mirror trying on their clothes. We laughed when we saw a TOO big lady trying to squeeze into a TOO little dress.

Later, after all our shopping was done, Mom took us to Bailey's for a big ice cream sundae. We rested our feet before we took the bus home.

This Saturday we went shopping for food. We got off the bus in the North End. First Mom took us to Haymarket to buy fruits and vegetables. Vinnie got mad when Mom squeezed the tomatoes (but she did anyway).

We went from cart to cart buying
everything—cantaloupes, bananas,
tomatoes, eggplant, lettuce, and onions.
My mother haggled until she got the
best price. Our bags got so heavy.

Next we walked to Alberto's Butcher Shop.

"Pound the cutlets nice and thin,"
my mom said, "and trim off all the fat."
   The butcher shop floor was covered with
sawdust. We sat on the step stool and
played with the cat while Mom and Alberto
talked in Italian.

We didn't know what they were saying, but they laughed a lot. And before we left, Alberto wiped his hands on his apron and gave us each a pinch on the cheek.

"*Belle!*" he said.

Our last stop was the bakery. We bought warm, homemade pizza, which we ate right away. Then, of course, we ordered four cannoli. We watched as Rosina squeezed the fresh cream into the crispy shells and gently put them in a box. "Don't tie it," Mom reminded her.

Pizzelle
Biscotti

Mom looked at her watch. We put down our heavy bags while we waited for the bus. We smiled when we saw our favorite bus driver, Bill.

We hurried to the back of the bus and
opened the box of cannoli. We scooped
out the cream, then ate the crunchy crust.
Over the bridge we went.